DEDICATION

To my brother Jim, who let go too soon,

and my husband Keith, who held on through the storm

ACKNOWLEDGEMENTS

First and foremost I'd like to thank Karen Stuth of Satiama Writers Resource, whose expert consultation guided me through all the phases of bringing Hold On, Toby to fruition, and to Sue Lion, whose creative illustrations brought Toby to life. Without them *Hold On, Toby* would remain but a dream.

A big thank-you to my dear friends Lynne Komraus and Lori Parsons who gave their time and attention to critiquing *Hold On, Toby* during the early revision process, and to Kitty Ramey for her patience and technical expertise in creating the video to market *Hold On, Toby*.

Boundless appreciation goes to my "champions" for their diligent participation in my crowd-funding campaign: Rick Bierbower, Jessica Noon, Kathi Johnson, Elaine Moore, Lynne Komraus, Lori Parsons, and the Boucher clan: KB & Janice, Nick & Anita, Don & Roxanne, Kathy, Carl & Cheryl.

Special thanks to my dad Carroll Bierbower, and to my friend and writing buddy Joe King, for their influence, encouragement and support, and to fellow authors in the Venice Writers Group whose varied input helped me to see new aspects of my story.

Last, but never least, much gratitude to many unnamed others who contributed in various ways to the reality of *Hold On, Toby*.

Hold On, Toby

Janet Bierbower-Boucher
Illustrated by Susan Andra Lion

At the edge of the great woods that surrounded a grassy green meadow stood a very big tree. Little leaf bud Toby curled up tightly against his branch of the very big tree. He grew there with hundreds of other leaf buds, all hugging the many branches that grew from their very big tree.

Spring sunbeams shone upon Toby giving him the strength to stretch and uncurl into a pale green leaf. Warm rain sprinkled on him, and upon the branch of the very big tree he grew bigger and stronger.

Big people admired the first flowers of spring that blossomed near the very big tree. Little people flew brightly colored kites across the fresh spring meadow.

One day a wiggly striped caterpillar crawled across Toby and nodded,

"Hold on! The best is yet to be."

"**I** wonder what the wiggly striped caterpillar means," Toby thought.

The days grew longer and the summer sun slowly changed Toby from a pale green color into a bright dark green.

Soon brilliant green leaves
fluttered on the many branches
of the very big tree. Only
small patches of blue sky
could peek through.

Big people unpacked a picnic basket
in the shade of the very big tree's leaves.
Little people ran barefoot, playing tag
on the tickly grass of the green meadow.

One evening a soft breeze murmured to Toby,

"Hold on! You will seeeeee!"

"I wonder what the soft breeze means,"
Toby thought.

Summer was ending. The days became shorter
and the nights cooler. Toby and all the other
leaves began to lose their bright green color.

One night Jack Frost spread a

chilly

cover upon Toby and promised,

"Hold on! Tomorrow you will be the best you can be."

"I wonder what Jack Frost means," Toby thought.

In the morning Toby's fading green color had turned into a blazing scarlet red.

Big people and little people marveled at Toby and all the leaves glistening in the sun,

proudly displaying their
spectacular colors.

The autumn wind whisked through the very big tree, whipping up all the leaves. It was hard for Toby to hold on.

"Toooooo soooooon," the wind howled.

"I wonder what the autumn wind means," Toby thought.

A stormy rain fell tap, tap, tapping on Toby.
"Not yet, not yet,"
the raindrops pleaded.

"**I** wonder what the stormy
raindrops mean," Toby thought.

Suddenly a big

blustery

gust of wind swept up and
grabbed Toby.

NOW!
commanded Mother Nature.

Toby finally understood what everyone meant. **He let go of the branch!**

Wheeeee he squealed,

dancing to and fro with the other leaves,

whirling and twirling as they drifted to the ground.

Big people raked Toby and all the fallen leaves into a nice neat pile.

Little people ran and jumped onto the pile,
tumbling Toby and the other leaves into the brisk air.

The days and nights became crispy cold.
Snowflakes floated down from the gray winter sky.

Big people helped little people build a funny
snowman in the snow white meadow.

All winter Toby and
the other leaves lay quietly under a blanket of fluffy
white snow that sparkled in the winter sun.

They became part of the earth...

feeding the roots of the very big tree.

The days grew warm again
and the snow melted.

Hundreds of
new little leaf buds
curled up tightly
against the many
branches that
grew from the
very big tree

that stood at the edge
of the great woods

that surrounded the
grassy green meadow.

If you listen carefully
you might hear
the soft whisper of the wind
in the sweet spring air,
"Hold on!
The best is yet to be."

Published 2016 by Windy Island Publishing, LLC
Email: windyislandp@gmail.com
Distributed by Satiama, LLC
www.satiama.com

ISBN: 978-0-692-66457-5
Library of Congress Number: 2016904829

Written by Janet Bierbower-Boucher
Illustrated by Susan Andra Lion
Book Design by Susan Andra Lion
Editing by Karen L Stuth, Satiama Writers Resource

Windy Island
PUBLISHING

PRINTED IN CHINA